The Woodland Gang Mysteries
by Irene Schultz

1. The Hidden Jewels
2. The Dark Old House
3. The Two Lost Boys
4. The Missing Will
5. The Stolen Animals
6. The Old Gold Coins
7. The Mystery Quilt
8. The Secret Spy Code
9. The Museum Robbery
10. The Ghost Cat
11. The Indian Cave
12. The Dinosaur Bones

The Woodland Gang

and THE GHOST

CAT

by Irene Schultz

Illustrated by Cindy Kahoun

Book 10 of the Series

ADDISON-WESLEY PUBLISHING COMPANY
Reading, Massachusetts • Menlo Park, California
New York • Don Mills, Ontario • Wokingham, England
Amsterdam • Bonn • Sydney • Singapore • Tokyo
Madrid • San Juan

To Isabel Slusser, a brave new U.S. citizen.

Created by BLACK and WHITE and READ ALL OVER Publishing Co.
Lake Bluff, Illinois 60044

Library of Congress Cataloging-in-Publication Data

Schultz, Irene, 1927–
The Woodland Gang and the *ghost cat.*

(The Woodland Gang mysteries; book 10)
Summary: On a camping trip to Cave Parka the Woodland Gang solve the mystery of their stolen food when they discover a "ghost cat" in a cave, which leads them to a family of Vietnamese refugees who are living in the cave.
1. Mystery and detective stories 2. Orphans—Fiction.
3. Caves—Fiction.
I. Title. II. Series: Schultz, Irene, 1927– . Woodland Gang mysteries; book 10.
PZ7.S3878Ws 1988 [Fic] 87-92260

ISBN 0-201-50054-X
2 3 4 5 6 7 8 9 10-WZ-96 95 94 93 92

Table of Contents

I—Rained Out

CHUBBY TEN-YEAR old Sammy woke up. He got out of his sleeping bag.

He stood up and stuck his head out of the big tent.

He said, "Oh Rats! Why did it have to rain? The first day of our camping trip!"

He made a face like a mad bull dog.

He said, "We drove all this way just to get rained on!"

His brother, Bill Westburg, fourteen, said, "Oh well, don't worry, Sammy. Maybe it will stop soon.

"We have a lot of games with us. We can have fun any way. At least we have a warm, dry place to stay."

Tall, skinny Mrs. Tandy, their house keeper, rolled over and sat up.

She said, "Warm and dry! That's what you think! My sleeping bag is all wet!"

"Wet?" Dave Briggs called from his cot.

"Just a minute 'til I get into my chair. I'll help you."

Dave was sixteen, blond and good-looking. He could not walk. But he did every thing else.

He lived with the Westburgs and Mrs. Tandy back in Bluff Lake. He had driven them to Cave Park in his car with hand controls.

The five of them called them selves the Woodland Gang.

Dave pulled him self into his wheel chair.

By then little Kathy Westburg, thirteen, was awake. She jumped out of her sleeping bag.

In her bare feet she ran over to Mrs. Tandy.

She was shy. Most of the time she didn't talk much. But now she said, "There's cold water all over this part of the tent floor! My feet are freezing!"

Her thin legs were shaking from the cold.

They all helped Mrs. Tandy put her

sleeping bag in a dry place.

Bill's friendly brown face looked worried.

He said, "Look, gang, this is pretty bad. There's water spreading to this corner, too.

"My guess is, we put up the tent on a dry river bed. Now it's running with water from the rain."

Sammy said, "The weather man said it would be warm! But I'm cold as a snow man!

"Hey!" he went on. "Listen! What's that noise?"

By then the others could hardly hear him.

Mrs. Tandy yelled, "That's the wind blowing louder! And the rain's coming down like a water fall!"

Just then they heard a loud CRACK! Some thing heavy fell out side the tent.

Bill looked out. "There is a big tree lying on the ground. Lucky it didn't fall on our tent!"

Dave yelled, "We are going to have to find a safer place. Even the station wagon would be better than this tent."

Sammy yelled, "But how can we pack up the tent in this rain?"

His eyes crossed. They always did when he was excited or tired.

His hair stuck out like a bunch of wild weeds.

All the Westburg children had been adopted. But now their mother and father were dead.

So Bill acted like a father. After all, he was four years older than Sammy.

He patted Sammy on the back. "It's OK, Sammy. We will leave the tent right here."

Dave yelled, "Just grab your things and head for the car."

They dressed in a rush.

They put on rain coats.

They made two trips to load up.

The wild wind blew water down their necks.

Sammy said, "Now I know what a bug in a river feels like."

Dave said, "Let's drive further into the park, to the park motel."

He pulled him self into the car. Bill got the wheel chair in. They started off.

The rain almost kept them from seeing.

It took them an hour to get there. But when they got to the motel, it was full. They could not stay.

They began to drive the miles back out of the park. The rain began to fall harder. All of a sudden Dave stopped the car, FAST!

Sammy shot forward, but his seat belt saved him.

He yelled, "What are you trying to do? Test the darn belt?"

Then they all saw why Dave had stopped.

A giant-size tree lay across the road.

Sammy said, "Holy Cats! We drove three hundred miles to get to Cave Park!

"We haven't even seen a cave.

"We are rained out of our tent.

"We are in the middle of a tornado!

"And we're trapped in our car! Some vacation!

"What do we do now?"

II—The New Camp

DAVE OPENED HIS window to look out. Then he closed it fast.

He said, "We have to move the car. This part of the road is low and muddy. We will get stuck if we stay here."

Bill said, "Can you back up a way? The road was higher back there."

Dave tried to back up.

The car tires flew around in the mud. The car wouldn't move.

Dave said, "We are stuck already."

Bill said, "Wait a minute. Sammy and I will get out and push."

Bill was short for fourteen. Sammy was nearly as tall as he. Both boys were fat and strong.

They jumped out into the rain.

Like two hardy ponies they stepped into the thick mud.

They pushed on the front of the station wagon. The car moved backward in the road. Mud shot out from under the tires. It shot all over their hands and rain coats.

Sammy tried to jump away.

He slipped. He landed face down in the mud.

Bill ran over to him and picked him up. He couldn't keep from smiling. Sammy's face was full of mud.

Sammy got mad. He said, "Stop laughing at me, you dumb brat baby."

Then he wiped both his hands over Bill's face. And both boys began laughing so hard they nearly fell in the mud again.

Then they both got back into the car.

Dave slowly backed up. There was no place to turn around. The rain kept pouring down.

Then suddenly Bill yelled, "Hey! Stop backing up, Dave!"

Dave said, "What's wrong?"

Bill said, "There's a road off to the right."

Every one tried to look through the rain to where Bill was pointing. They saw a tiny road that went up into the woods.

Dave drove onto the road. He said, "Maybe this will take us to higher ground."

The road DID keep going up hill.

After fifteen minutes it was Sammy who yelled, "STOP THE CAR! Look at that! Look over at those big rocks!"

Dave stopped the car.

They all looked through the rain. They saw a big sign on a chain between two posts.

It said, THE DEVIL'S DEEP FREEZE CHAIN OF CAVES.

THIS CAVE NOT IN USE.
MAPS BEING MADE.

In back of the sign was a big black hole in the rocks.

Sammy yelled, "A cave! I want to see it."

He opened the car door. He jumped right out in the rain.

He ran behind the sign and into the cave.

Bill jumped out and ran after him. He yelled, "Sammy! Watch out! You don't know what's in there!"

Kathy and Mrs. Tandy pulled Dave's chair out of the station wagon.

Then they helped him through the rain to the cave.

He wheeled inside onto a smooth dry stone floor.

There stood Bill and Sammy.

They were looking at one side of the

cave. Even in the near dark every one could see things sticking out of the floor and ceiling.

Dave had his flash light. He turned it on.

Sammy said, "Hey! Look at that!"

Mrs. Tandy said, "How beautiful!"

Thousands of long pieces of shiny rock hung down from the ceiling, like thick icicles.

Thousands more stuck up from the floor.

In some places the top ones and bottom ones touched.

Sammy said, "Holy Hot Dogs! What IS all THAT!"

Dave said, "The ones on the ceiling are called sta—lac—tites.

"The ones on the floor are called sta—lag—mites."

Kathy said, "My teacher told us how you can remember which is which. Sta—lac—tite has a letter 'c' in it. She says that 'c' is for ceiling."

Bill said, "I can tell you some thing your teacher didn't know."

Dave asked, "What's that?"

Bill said, "We are standing in a perfect place to sleep tonight."

Sammy said, "What kind of a dopey idea is that?"

Kathy said, "It's not so dopey, Sammy.

At least it's dry here."

Sammy said, "But it's so dark."

Dave said, "We have three lanterns with us. And our flash lights."

Mrs. Tandy said, "It's safe, too. A tree won't fall on us in here."

Sammy said, "But we will need water to drink. I'm thirsty right now!"

Dave said, "We have enough drinking water in the car for twenty-four hours. But we won't have any for washing unless we can trap some rain water in some thing."

Sammy said, "That settles it! Let's stay here! Nobody will have to wash for one full day and night. And besides we can explore the cave."

Kathy was shy, but she loved adventure. She said, "That's a great idea. The sign didn't say danger or keep out. It just said the cave was being mapped.

"I wish we could stay for more than a day!"

Dave said, "I bet we will have this part of the park all to our selves. Did you notice the road has grass growing on it? That means no one uses it much."

Mrs. Tandy said, "My Word, gang. What are we waiting for? It looks like it's time to unload the station wagon. The Woodland Gang is moving into it's new camping place."

III—The Devil's Deep Freeze

BILL AND KATHY brought the sleeping bags into the cave.

Mrs. Tandy and Dave brought in the suit cases.

Sammy was always hungry.

He called, "I'm bringing the food boxes first!"

In ten minutes the car was empty.

And the rain had washed most of the mud off of Sammy and Bill.

A pile of camping things sat inside of the cave.

Bill lit a lantern and put it on a high rock.

It lit all of the walls of the cave.

Sammy said, "This cave is BIG, big as a house! We can fix it up. It will be fun. But first, how about breakfast!"

Dave said, "That's a good idea. Now where should we keep the food?"

Sammy said, "Let's have this big flat rock be our kitchen."

Bill said, "Fine! I can set up our cooking pots on it. And here's our camp stove."

He lit the stove while Sammy unpacked the cans and bags of food.

Kathy hung Mrs. Tandy's sleeping bag over some stalagmites to dry.

Then she laid out the other sleeping bags. The rest of the gang made the food.

Mrs. Tandy opened two packages of chicken hot dogs. That made sixteen hot dogs.

She put some of their water into a pot.

Bill put the hot dogs on to boil.

Bill said, "This is breakfast and lunch, together. We're having brunch. So let's see what else we can add to it."

Dave unpacked a loaf of bread, and the mustard.

He took lettuce out of a plastic bag.

Sammy dug out the big bag of fruit. He found five big oranges.

Then he found the oat meal cookies in plastic bags. He took out ten of those. "Lucky we made four batches of cookies," he said. "We're going to need a lot of energy for exploring."

Bill found their paper plates, and their napkins and paper cups.

He said, "The more I think of it, the more I like camping in this cave. Let's eat fast, and have a look around."

Dave said, "I wonder how it got its name, Devil's Deep Freeze? It doesn't seem cold to me. But there's a sign inside the cave opening that says the same name."

When they were done eating, there were two hot dogs left over.

They left them on a plate with plastic over it, on the kitchen rock.

They put all their garbage into a box near the cave opening.

Then they began to explore with their flash lights.

Sammy said, "This cave is about as big as the movie house back home. It's a giant!"

Dave said, "Look at these stalactites and stalagmites that meet each other.

"They are made like icicles, from water dripping down.

"The water will carry different kinds of rock dust in it. That dust turns hard.

"Some of the rock dust drips to the floor and starts building upward. After thousands of years, the upper and lower parts of the dripping may meet."

Mrs. Tandy said, "Some of these rock shapes remind me of trees."

Bill said, "Or giant sand castles."

Bill and Sammy pushed Dave in his chair among the stalagmites.

Kathy said, "This is like a fairy land, but it scares me a little. Every time we move our flash lights, the shadows move."

Dave said, "Don't be afraid. Stay near me, Kathy." He took hold of her hand.

Kathy's face turned red. Then she tripped on a little stalagmite. But she didn't take her hand away.

Slowly they walked around the whole cave.

Suddenly Bill said, "Hey! I hear water running."

Every one stood still.

Kathy said, "I hear it too. It's coming from the wall near me. She shined her light around.

"Wait! In back of this bunch of stalagmites! There's an opening!"

Sammy ran over. He flashed his light there too.

He said, "Holy Cow! There's a BIG opening! It goes in and bends a little. Like a hall way!"

He stepped through it. Bill ran through after him.

The others could hear their voices.

"Good Grief!" Sammy yelled.

"It's beautiful!" Bill called. "Come on in, gang. Water. And another cavern!"

Sammy said, "What's a cav—ern?"

Bill said, "It's a large cave room."

They all went through the stone hall way.

The second room of the cave was as big as the first one.

On the far wall was a tall water fall. It began way up near the ceiling.

The water fell into a small pool at the bottom.

Dave said, "I bet this water is pure and clean. I think we could drink it.

"And Bill and Sammy, you can get your hair washed out in the pool. You've still got mud in it from your car-pushing."

Bill said, "That means we really could camp in this cave for our whole trip."

Sammy was on his knees. He was shining his flash light into the pool.

"Hey!" he said. "I'm not putting my head in this pool. Some thing's living in it already!"

Every one looked in. Sure enough, little white fish were swimming back and forth.

Dave said, "I've read about those. I never thought I'd be lucky enough to see one."

"What's so good about them?" Sammy asked.

Dave said, "Look at their eyes! There's skin over them. These are blind cave fish.

"They're in the dark all the time, so they can live here even without eyes."

Bill said, "There must be some thing else strange about this cave, too. The Devil's Deep Freeze name must mean some thing."

Mrs. Tandy said, "Let's take a walk around this cavern. Let's look for a rock shaped like a freezer maybe."

Sammy said, "Or we could find an ice-making machine, maybe."

Bill said, "That's the most goofy idea you've had yet."

Sammy got mad. His eyes crossed. "It was a joke," he said. "You don't know a joke when you hear one."

He made his hands into fists.

His hair got all wild.

Bill said, "OK, Sammy, OK. I'm sorry if I hurt your feelings. I thought you really meant it. I didn't know it was a joke."

Dave had wheeled a little further around the cave room.

Suddenly he yelled, "Hey, come look at this. It isn't a joke! Feel this wall."

They all ran over to where he was. They shined their lights on the wall. Some things like strips of glass were hanging on it.

Bill touched one. "Holy Bananas!" he yelled. "This wall is covered with strips of ice.

"It IS an ice-making machine. THIS is the Devil's Deep Freeze. And it's freezing in the middle of summer!"

IV—The Missing Hot Dogs

SAMMY SAID, "SEE, smarty pants Billy brat baby, see! I KNEW there was an ice-maker here!"

Bill said, "I thought you said you were

just making a joke."

Sammy said, "I knew what the Devil's Deep Freeze was, all the time."

Dave laughed. He said, "Come on, gang. Let's see what else we can find in this place. Maybe we can discover WHY there's ice here, even in summer.

"Come on, Kathy, let's lead the way."

Kathy ran over to him. She thought Dave was the smartest and nicest boy she had ever met.

She was shy with most people. And she tried to hide the braces on her teeth, too.

But Dave was so friendly and interesting, she forgot to be shy with him.

She walked next to him. She shined her light so he could wheel his chair.

Half way around they came to another opening. Sammy said, "Let's go in!"

Dave said, "We shouldn't go any further until we go back for lanterns!"

Mrs. Tandy said, "Inside that opening, it's the blackest black I've ever seen. Not a bit of light comes through from the first cavern."

Sammy said, "Let's all turn our flash lights out and see what it's like when no one is here."

The others all said OK.

Bill added, "Just do it for a few seconds."

Sammy said, "What's wrong? Are you afraid?"

Bill said, "Well, I know I won't like it."

Sammy said, "Aw, come on, scared-y-cat. When I say NOW, let's do it.

"NOW!"

The entire cave went black.

Then a scared voice said, "Bill, where are you?"

It was Sammy. HE was the scared one! Bill reached out until he touched Sammy.

He said, "Turn on your light, Sammy," and he turned his on.

Sammy said, "I didn't want to be the first. You'd think I was a scared-y-cat, like I said about you."

Bill said, "Come on, Sammy. I wouldn't care if you WERE afraid of inky blackness.

"Every one is afraid of some thing. That's no big deal.

"Let's go back for the lanterns, gang."

Back they went across the second cavern, into the first cave room.

Their lantern was burning brightly.

Bill said, "Here I'll light another one. We can leave this one where it is."

Kathy said, "I'm afraid we might walk so far, we'll forget how to get back . . . like Becky and Tom in the cave . . . in the book *Tom Sawyer*."

Mrs. Tandy said, "I've got an idea, if you think it would work.

"Remember in that old Greek story? When the hero found his way out of a monster's cave? He had some string that he followed.

"Well, how about my balls of yarn? I brought them to knit a sweater. But I'd rather explore than knit!"

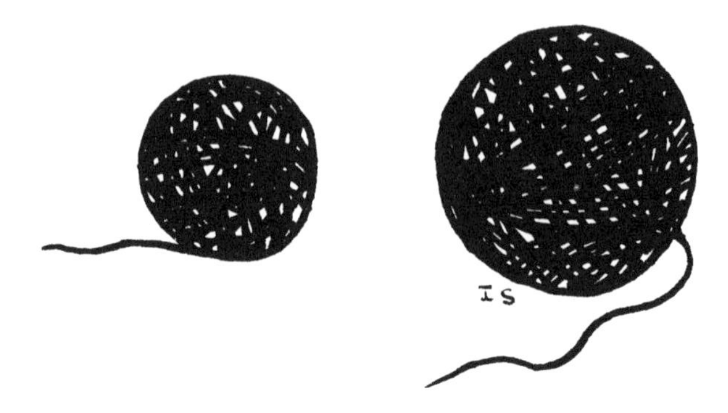

She got one ball from her bag.

"Hooray," said Sammy. "Now I'll just get one of our left-over hot dogs to eat for energy, and we're ready."

Bill went to the cave door. "It's still terrible out," he said. "No one could travel in weather like this."

Mrs. Tandy said, "We are snug as five bugs in a rug! We can explore all we want, and no one can even get near our cave in this storm."

Just then Sammy came walking away from the kitchen rock.

He carried a piece of plastic in one hand.

He carried a paper plate in the other.

He had a very funny look on his face.

Mrs. Tandy said, "What's wrong, honey? Weren't the hot dogs any good?"

Sammy said, "You're not going to believe this! I didn't eat the hot dogs . . . because they were gone.

"Some one came into our cave. He ate the hot dogs while we were exploring.

"And what if he's still in here?"

V—The White Thing

THE WOODLAND GANG all stood perfectly still.

Every one's heart was pounding. The black shadows all around the rocks in the cave seemed bigger and darker. Some one could be hiding in any one of them.

Kathy whispered, "W-w-what should we do?"

Her knees felt weak.

She had hold of Bill's arm, and she felt like fainting.

Dave said, "Let's not panic. If some one is in this cave, he's probably here because he's lost. Or he needed to get out of the storm, like us."

Bill said, "Dave's right. Let's find out who it is.

"HELLO THERE," he called. "WHO IS IN THIS CAVE?"

". . . in this cave," came an echo of Bill's voice.

Dave called, "IF YOU'RE HERE, COME OUT! WE WON'T HURT YOU."

". . . won't hurt you," the echo answered Dave.

They waited.

At last Sammy whispered, "First I hope some one will answer. Then I hope no one will answer."

Mrs. Tandy whispered, "Me too. NOW what do we do? I feel like running."

Dave said, "Just a minute, Sammy. I have an idea."

He reached out. "Let me see that plate and plastic, will you? Where did you find them?"

Sammy said, "By the side of our kitchen rock, on the ground. The plastic was in one place, sort of torn. The plate was a few feet away."

Dave opened out the plastic.

He looked at it carefully. "It's torn into little strips here," he said.

Bill said, "Look at those four little pin pricks in it over there."

Kathy said, "Why would a person do all that just to unwrap it?"

Dave said, "A person would NOT do this to unwrap it. I bet I know why we didn't get an answer when we yelled."

Bill said, "I bet I know what you're thinking! We were yelling at an animal!"

"An animal?" said Sammy. "You mean some stinky little pest ate my hot dogs?"

"Well," said Dave, "I hope it wasn't a stinky pest. We couldn't fight a skunk for this cave.

"But it is a little animal. You can see how close together his claw marks are."

Kathy said, "It's almost the size of a cat's paw, but I don't think a cat would live in a cave."

"Oh Boy!" said Sammy. "Maybe it's a wild cat."

Bill said, "Come on, Sammy. The paw that tore this plastic is little. Wild cats are pretty big."

Sammy said, "Then maybe it's a BABY wild cat. Or a raccoon. Or a wood chuck. Or a giant squirrel. Or a monkey. Or a monster cave frog like the seven pound ones in Africa. Or a . . ."

By then Kathy was smiling a little.

The others began to laugh.

Then even Sammy began to giggle.

Bill said, "We'll find the little pest. Here's what we'll do.

"I'll light all three lanterns. We'll leave one here, and carry two.

"We'll search this first room of the cave.

"Then we'll leave the second lantern in the hall way.

"What ever the animal is, if it's wild it will be afraid to come past this light.

"We'll do the same in any new room of the cave. We'll just keep bringing the two lanterns forward by turns."

Mrs. Tandy said, "I'll just tie this yarn around a stalagmite here. Then we will be all set for our cave walk.

"And Bill," she went on, "would you take our bag of meat? We may as well keep it fresh at the Deep Freeze."

Sammy said, "I'll put our pop cans in the fish pond. It's good and cold, and they won't hurt the fish."

So the gang started their animal hunt.

They looked behind every stalagmite and rock in the first cavern.

They looked on top of every rock too.

They could see nothing.

They walked into the second cavern.

Mrs. Tandy let out yarn as they walked.

They looked over every inch of that cavern.

No luck.

Bill went to the new opening with the third lantern.

He said, "Now, Kathy, bring that other one over to explore with."

Sammy said, "I saw some thing once in a TV movie. This man was in a dark cave and wanted to make sure there were no holes he might fall into.

"So he stood in the door way of each new cavern, and threw some stones to test the floor, like this."

Sammy picked up some stones from the floor near him. He threw a handful into the cave room they were looking into.

Then they heard a terrible SCREAM!

Some thing white flew through the air and disappeared in the darkness.

Mrs. Tandy dropped her ball of wool.

"Holy COW!" yelled Bill.

He grabbed Dave's chair. "COME ON GANG!"

And the whole Woodland Gang ran through both cavern rooms.

They ran out into the heavy rain.

They dashed into the station wagon.

They locked the car doors. They were soaking wet.

Sammy said, "That was a ghost! A screaming ghost. You always said there were no ghosts, Bill."

He socked Bill's arm. "You lied to me."

Bill said, "I still say there are no ghosts." But his voice shook a little.

They sat there for a full minute, shaking.

Then some thing strange happened. Mrs. Tandy began to laugh.

Bill said, "What's wrong? How come you're laughing? Are you OK, Mrs. Tandy?"

Mrs. Tandy said, "Never felt better. I just realized what our screaming ghost was. I know what it was that we all ran away from!"

VI—A Mama Ghost

Mrs. Tandy said, "I bet it was a cat!"

"A cat!" they all said.

Dave said, "That terrible noise was from a cat?"

Mrs. Tandy said, "My, yes. I've had lots

of cats in my day. I was just so frightened, I wasn't thinking. Other wise I'd have known right away it was a cat.

"I remember I once stepped on my cat Punky's tail. She screamed just like that. She took off like a bird, too."

Kathy said, "Why, the poor thing. One of the stones must have hit it."

Sammy said, "Boy, I feel like a rat. I didn't mean to hit it. I wouldn't hurt a cat."

Mrs. Tandy said, "We know that, Sammy."

Sammy said, "But what if it isn't a cat? I still think it sounded like a screaming ghost."

Bill said, "Ghosts don't fly around eating hot dogs, Sammy. I bet it was the cat that ate our hot dogs."

Dave said, "Suppose I get back into my chair. Then we'll go and see what's really in there."

Back into the cave they went. They put on dry clothes. They looked through the first two caverns. No cat.

Kathy said, "Do you think he will still be there . . . in the third cavern?"

Bill said, "I suppose he may have sneaked out side in the rain. We were in the car for a few minutes."

Dave said, "It's so wet, he'd have come back."

Bill said, "Let me get some thing. I'll be back in a minute."

He ran over to the icy wall.

He opened a new package of hot dogs. They weren't frozen yet.

He handed a hot dog to Mrs. Tandy.

He said, "Here, you know about cats. Maybe you can get him to come out if you use this. He must have liked the other two hot dogs he took."

The gang walked into the third cave room.

Mrs. Tandy called, "Here kitty, kitty, kitty."

They walked all around.

Mrs. Tandy held the hot dog out in front of her and kept calling.

The second time around, they heard a noise near the back of the cavern.

"Meow."

"Hey, did you hear that?" asked Bill. "I think it came from those rocks in that corner."

They moved slowly toward the rocks.

Mrs. Tandy called again softly, "Here kitty, kitty, kitty."

A second "Meow," answered her.

They got to the rocks.

Here is what they saw.

A low place in some rocks made a hard nest. It was filled with soft green leaves.

In the middle of the leaves sat a pure white cat.

Under her feet lay four little kittens!

Sammy called out, "Oh, it's a SHE! Not a he. And she doesn't look hurt at all. And look at the babies!"

Mrs. Tandy said, "How darling! Look, their eyes are open. They must be at least a week old!"

Kathy said, "Hi, you pretty ghost cat! Here, have a piece of hot dog."

She broke off a piece from the hot dog

Mrs. Tandy held.

She held it out to the cat.

At first the cat just sat still. She was afraid of them.

Then she leaned forward to smell the food.

Kathy held it closer.

At last the cat took it in her mouth and chewed it up.

Kathy gave her another piece. She said, "Here Mama Ghost, you need to eat a lot. You have to make milk to feed your children."

Kathy patted the cat's head and neck. She said, "You are a wonderful cat."

Sammy said, "Hey, Kathy, you talk more to this cat than you do to me! Let me pat her!"

He rubbed his hand down her back. She lay down in her rock nest.

The kittens crawled against her body. They began to drink from her.

Sammy kept petting her.

A funny noise came out of her chest.

Sammy said, "Hey, Ghosty, you're purring. You like me, don't you?"

He turned to the others.

"Can we keep her? Let's take her back to Bluff Lake when we go home. She likes me already. I'll take care of her and the babies."

Mrs. Tandy said, "I don't see why not. When we are all set to go, why not take her?"

Kathy said, "Mop may not like having cats around."

Mop was their little tan dog. They had left him with their friends at home.

Bill said, "Mop is such a scared-y-cat. He'd probably faint if he saw a cat."

Sammy said, "Then we can keep the cats in the basement until they're older. We will give the kittens away and keep Ghosty."

Kathy said, "The vet can fix her so she won't keep having kittens. Oh let's keep her."

Bill said, "It's fine with me. I think she's a great cat.

"She found a place to have her babies.

"She did it all alone.

"She keeps them clean as new shoes.

"She finds food for her self, and feeds them.

"Let's keep her."

Dave said, "Ghosty is a great cat. But there's just some thing I don't understand about this."

Bill asked, "What's that, Dave?"

Dave said, "How come this cat is so fat if she's taking care of her self?"

Sammy said, "I've heard of cats and dogs that could take care of them selves. Didn't you ever read *The Incredible Journey*?"

"Yes," Dave answered, "but here's another thing. Did any one ever hear about a cat being able to pick fresh leaves to make a soft nest?"

Mrs. Tandy said, "My word, Dave! I never have."

Dave said, "Then how did all those leaves get into Ghosty's nest? That's a mystery!"

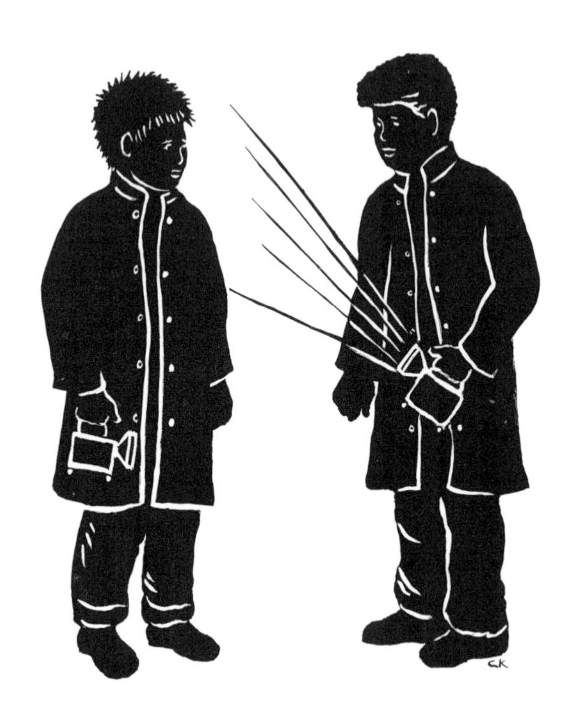

VII—The Missing Pets

Bill said, "Let's give the rest of that hot dog to Ghosty. Then let's go back to our camping cavern."

Sammy said, "I'm hungry too. Cats aren't the only ones people should give hot dogs to!" He sounded cross and tired.

Mrs. Tandy said, "Why Sammy, no wonder you're hungry! You poor dear. It's five o'clock already."

Dave said, "I can't WAIT until the chief gets here tomorrow, and hears about this."

"Good Grief!" Mrs. Tandy said. "That's right! He plans to meet us at the first camp ground at noon. Now we are flooded out of there. How will he find us?"

Chief Hemster was head of the police in Bluff Lake.

He was a good friend of the Woodland Gang. He was driving 300 miles to camp with them.

Dave said, "We will have to drive to the tent tomorrow."

Kathy looked worried. She said, "What if they haven't moved that tree from across the road?"

Dave said, "Then some of us will climb over it and walk to meet him. Don't worry, Kathy. We will get there."

Bill said, "This is a national park. I'll bet the road is open already, right now."

Sammy said, "OK, then here's an IMPORTANT thing to worry about . . . What's for dinner?"

Bill got the camp stove burning.

Mrs. Tandy said, "Take out two cans of soup from that box, Sammy. Let's mix them together and see what we get."

Sammy took chicken vegetable, and mushroom soup.

He put them into a big pot.

He added two cans of water.

Mrs. Tandy said, "We can have eggs, or canned chicken, too. I don't suppose you want more hot dogs again. What will it be?"

"HOT DOGS!" every one said.

So Bill got some more hot dogs and put them into the soup to heat up.

Soon the soup began to steam.

Dave said, "Look, the steam is blowing away from the mouth of the cave."

Bill said, "I saw that at lunch, too."

Mrs. Tandy said, "It moves into the next cavern. Fast, too, like smoke up a chimney."

Dave said, "I think that means some thing interesting. Some where in these caverns there's another opening to the out side."

Kathy said, "But Dave. It couldn't be in any of the three caverns we've been in. We'd have seen some light coming in."

Bill said, "Maybe not, Kathy. Remember how dark it is out side from the storm?"

Dave said, "Well, suppose we hunt for it tomorrow."

Bill said, "We can bring a few sticks of dead wood in side. They would dry out a little tonight.

"Then we can set fire to them tomorrow. We can follow the smoke they give off, to find the other opening."

Mrs. Tandy said, "I left my ball of yarn in the cat cave.

"When we start exploring in the morning, I will keep letting more yarn out.

"Now our dinner's almost ready."

Bill and Sammy brought in some cold pop from the blind-fish pool.

Dave got out the bread and mustard again.

They used plastic bowls for their soup. They made sandwiches out of their hot dogs.

They wiped their soup bowls clean with pieces of bread. Then they ate the bread.

"Great dinner!" Sammy said. "I love our cave. I don't feel scared any more."

Bill said, "Me either. Let's go run water into these bowls. Then they will be washed and ready for breakfast."

Sammy said, "Good idea. We can do it at the water fall."

They took a lantern. They walked into the second cavern.

Bill washed the bowls.

Then Sammy said, "Let's go in to see Ghosty.

"I'll take her another hot dog."

They walked into the third cave and over to the rock nest.

Sammy and Bill leaned over and looked inside.

Ghosty was not there.

The kittens were not there.

All that was left were the leaves.

They ran back and told the others.

The whole Woodland Gang looked every where in the cat cave for Ghosty and her kittens.

They walked behind every rock.

They shined their lantern up the walls.

They even shined their flash lights over the ceiling.

At last Dave said, "Let's call it quits for tonight."

Sammy looked as if he were ready to cry.

Bill said, "Sammy, I promise you we will find Ghosty tomorrow, or I'll get you another cat back home."

They went back to the first cave to go to sleep.

They left the hot dog in Ghosty's empty nest.

During the night the hot dog disappeared.

VIII—The Chief Comes

THE NEXT MORNING the Woodland Gang woke up late.

Sammy had pulled his sleeping bag between Dave's and Bill's.

When Bill woke up, Sammy was holding his hand.

Bill shook Sammy's hand a little.

"Wake up, Sammy. It's nine o'clock already. It's time to hunt for Ghosty."

Sammy said, "Hey! Who put a rock under my sleeping bag?"

He pulled it out and dropped it onto Bill's stomach.

Quick as a cat, Bill rolled over, out of his sleeping bag right on top of Sammy.

"Stop throwing stones at me, you rotten little monkey!"

In a minute they were wrestling all over the cave floor, half mad, half laughing.

Then Dave said loudly, "IS THIS GOOD CEREAL!"

Bill and Sammy looked up. The rest of the gang were sitting around in their pajamas. They were eating instant oat meal.

Kathy was pouring milk into hers. She said, "Pass the brown sugar, please."

In a second the wrestlers stopped wrestling.

Sammy and Bill ran over for cereal.

Sammy had a big smile on his face. He said, "I love to wake up with a good wrestle."

Then he added, "Say, why is it so dark in here?"

He ran to the mouth of the cave.

"Holy Cats! It's still pouring rain out there!

"It's still black as night out."

Bill said, "Speaking of holy cats, it's time for the great cat hunt. Let's get dressed."

They got their clothes on in a hurry.

Dave said, "We looked all over the cat cavern for Ghosty last night. But we were tired. Let's start there again."

Back they went.

First they looked in the stone nest again.

Sammy said, "NOW I'M MAD! That sneaky, little Ghosty! The hot dog's gone! She's got to be around here some where."

But call and hunt as much as they

could, they couldn't find her.

At last Dave said, "We have to stop. It's ten o'clock.

"We have to meet Chief Hemster at the camp grounds. And we will have to drive as slowly as we did yesterday, in this rain.

"We'll hunt later, Sammy, when the chief is here. We KNOW that Ghosty is some where near by."

They put on their rain coats.

They made a mad dash to the station wagon.

They found the tree was not blocking the road any more.

The forest rangers had cut it on both ends.

They had pulled the middle part over to the side of the road.

The gang got to the camp grounds by eleven.

"Good heavens!" Mrs. Tandy said. "Look at our tent now!"

It was standing in about three inches of rushing water.

Just then they heard a car horn. HONK! HONK! HONK!

They saw the head lights of a car coming toward them.

It stopped next to them.

Out jumped Chief Hemster.

Kathy threw the station wagon door open. The chief jumped in with them.

"I got here earlier than I thought I would," he said.

"I left at four o'clock in the morning because I heard the weather would be bad.

"Are you all alright? Your tent looks a little like Noah's Ark."

Mrs. Tandy said, "We are fine, John. We've found the most wonderful place to stay. We will lead you there."

Sammy LOVED to tease Mrs. Tandy about Chief Hemster.

He said, "Mrs. Tandy will be GLAD to ride with you in your car. She'll show you the way. And you can hold her HAND!"

Chief Hemster reached forward and grabbed Sammy's nose.

"I think I'll hold THIS for a while, first," he laughed.

Then he said, "Come on Becky." The two of them jumped into his car.

An hour later they were all safely inside

of the cave.

The rain was still coming down in a flood out side.

They made hot instant lemonade to warm up.

Then they unloaded Chief Hemster's car.

After that they showed the chief all around the three caverns.

They showed him the ball of yarn . . . the water fall . . . the blind fish . . . the Devil's Deep Freeze.

They told him about the Ghost Cat . . . about the missing hot dogs . . . about the terrible scream . . . about the kittens.

They showed him the stone nest with the leaves still in it.

The chief said, "There HAS to be another cavern where Ghosty has gone. She wouldn't carry her babies out side in this storm.

"We'll hunt some more. But first let's

have lunch. I brought you a surprise."

He opened a big box. It was filled with fried chicken.

He opened a big bag. It had ears of corn in it.

He said, "Boil up some water with a little sugar in it. It only takes a few minutes to cook corn, once the water's ready."

Bill said, "Oh, we forgot to tell you about how the steam blows out to the next cavern."

Dave said, "We think there's another

hole from the caverns to the out side."

Sammy said, "Maybe that's where Ghosty and her kittens are . . . where ever that opening is."

Bill lit a big stick of wood on the camp stove.

He said, "Let's take a look at where the smoke goes, right now."

Mrs. Tandy said, "We have plenty of time while the water is coming to a boil."

They followed the smoke with their flash lights. They took their lanterns and the chief's lantern.

The smoke from the burning stick blew through the first cavern, and through the stone hall way.

It went into the second cavern and straight across.

"Good Grief!" said Dave. "It's disappearing against the top of that wall! Right behind the top of the water fall."

IX—The Secret of the Waterfall

"SAMMY SAID, "GHOSTY could never have carried her kittens up that rock wall and to the top of the water fall.

"How could she even pick them up?"

Mrs. Tandy said, "Oh, she could pick them up. I used to see my mother cat pick up her babies.

"She took their heads in her mouth. She lifted them carefully. They hung down like little bags. It didn't hurt them at all."

Dave said, "You're right though, Sammy. She couldn't take them way up there."

Bill had walked over to the left side of the water fall.

"Will you look at this!" he called.

Then he disappeared with his lantern.

Sammy shouted, "Hey, Bill! Where are you?"

"Right here," came an answer. It was Bill's voice. They could hardly hear him.

Then a second later he jumped out and was with them again.

They all ran to him.

"Come here," he said. "Look at what I found."

He pointed up and down, in back of the left side of the water fall.

The water at the top of the fall, shot forward. It did not run down the rock wall on that side.

It fell three feet in front of the wall.

Between the water and the wall went a stone path. And it led to a tall, wide crack in the stone behind the water fall. It was a huge opening, wider than a door way.

A person could easily walk right through it.

Bill said, "Ghosty did not have to carry her kittens up high where the smoke goes. She could just walk through here.

They all followed Bill through the wall.

They were in a cavern bigger than the first three.

Sammy stood with his mouth open.

For once in his life he couldn't say any thing. At last he whispered, "Holy Cow! This is the biggest room I've ever seen! You could hold a track meet in here."

Bill said, "You'd have to cut off about ten thousand stalagmites first, to smooth the floor."

Mrs. Tandy said, "This is fantastic! Let's explore it, right now."

Sammy said, "Remember your ball of yarn? I'll go get it. We'll bring it under the water fall. Then we won't get lost if we find ANOTHER cavern!"

The fourth cavern was almost round in shape.

Bill and Sammy helped push Dave over the stony floor.

Bill said, "I feel I'm in an under ground forest."

Kathy said, "So many stalactites hang almost to the floor. They do look like tree trunks."

Sammy said, "And look at all the water running in little streams all through this cavern. That's like in a forest too."

Kathy said, "Let's get over to the walls. Let's see if there are any other door ways into this room."

Dave said, "Good idea. I'll look around in the parts that are flat. You all go through the bumpy parts."

Bill said, "Sammy, come over here. The smoke stick has stopped burning. Let's see if we can get it lit again."

But they could not.

Bill said, "We'll have to look for the opening without it."

They climbed around the rocky places.

Suddenly Sammy said, "Hey, what's that big black hole above these rocks?"

He held his lantern high.

Five rocks lay behind each other.

They went higher and higher, like big crooked stairs.

The boys climbed them.

At the top was an opening in the wall. It was big enough to stand in.

Sammy and Bill looked inside.

They saw another cave room, like a second floor in a house.

Sammy was all ready to run into it.

Just then they heard a little far-off crying sound.

Sammy said, "Ghosty and her kittens are there some where. You can hear them. Let's go!"

Bill said, "No, Sammy. We have to go back."

He grabbed Sammy's arm.

Sammy said, "Let go of me!"

Bill said, "Listen to me, you monkey! We haven't even got the ball of yarn up here."

Sammy said, "You're always trying to boss me around, Billy brat baby. I won't go back!"

Bill suddenly changed his voice.

He stopped sounding bossy.

He said, "Too bad you don't want to go back, Sammy. It's time for lunch! Fried chicken and corn. But I guess you're not interested."

"I forgot," Sammy said. "I guess I need some food so I'll be better at exploring. But listen to those kittens."

Bill said, "Hurry, Sammy. Down the stones fast. That's it."

He called to the others, "I've left the corn water boiling. We'd better get back to the kitchen cave."

They wondered why he was in such a hurry, all of a sudden, but they all joined him.

He grabbed Dave. He almost ran with the chair over the bumpy floor.

They followed the yarn right out under the water fall.

He raced with Dave back to their kitchen cavern.

Dave said, "What's the hurry, Bill? I was afraid we were going to fly right through the water fall and land in the pool with the fish!"

Chief Hemster said, "What's wrong? Did some thing scare you?"

Sammy said, "I guess Bill was afraid he'd burn the water pot dry."

Kathy said, "Look!" She pointed at the camp stove. There was nothing cooking on it.

Dave said, "Holy Cow!"

Sammy said, "Hey! Where's our pot? Some one stole it. And our bag of corn! And it wasn't a cat that could do that!"

Bill whispered, "Stand close, every one. I have to tell you some thing.

"Sammy and I heard a crying in that upper cavern. Sammy thought it was the kittens.

"I'm sure it didn't sound like any kittens I've ever heard. I think it was a little kid crying. That's why I rushed us out."

Sammy's eyes crossed over almost to his nose. His hair stood up like a porcupine's.

He took hold of Bill's arm. "Good Grief!" he said. "What if the guy who stole our corn, stole some one's baby? What if there's a kid-napper hiding out in these caves?"

X—The Under Ground Lake

Mrs. Tandy said, "Good Heavens! What do we do next?"

Chief Hemster said, "Well, we have to check out that upper cavern, all together. No going off in pairs."

Dave said, "Look here, gang. I bet who ever is in the cave, is no kid-napper. He must be the owner of Ghosty. Kid-nappers don't run around with a cat and kittens. I bet he isn't even dangerous."

Sammy said, "Well, I'm going to eat some chicken before he steals that!"

He stuffed a chicken leg into his mouth. Then he ate up a wing.

Bill said, "You do make a lot of sense some times, Sammy," and he helped him self to a wing.

Dave said, "We do need to keep our selves strong to search the cave."

Then all of them dived into the fried chicken.

At last Mrs. Tandy said, "Here are some cookies for every one. Now let's go."

They headed for the water fall.

Bill led the way in back of it.

Chief Hemster came next, then Kathy and Mrs. Tandy. Sammy pushed Dave last.

They all took their flash lights.

Dave said, "Don't take the lanterns. We may run into some one. We might want to turn off the light in a hurry."

They came to the rock steps.

Bill whispered to Dave, "Some of us will go ahead for a minute. We've got to see what the cavern floor is like before we take you up there."

Chief Hemster, Kathy and Bill climbed the rock steps.

They shined their lights ahead.

They saw a huge cavern. It bent to the left. They could not see beyond the bend.

Kathy whispered down, "It's a smooth floor, the part we can see, Dave."

Dave said, "Then here I come. Don't try pulling me up, gang. It's too steep. I'll climb sitting down."

He pushed himself up out of his wheel chair onto the lowest stone.

He reached down to pick up one leg and then the other.

Now his feet were on the rock he was sitting on. Then he put his hands on the step behind him.

Sammy gave him a little lift, and Dave was on the next rock. One by one he moved up the rocks.

In a few minutes he was at the top. Sammy brought up his wheel chair. Dave lifted him self in.

They went through the first part of the cave very slowly.

They looked behind every rock and stalagmite.

Sammy whispered, "There are a million hiding places in this cavern. That corn-crook could jump out and grab us." His voice shook a little.

Bill patted his hand. "It's OK, Sammy," he whispered back. "I'll stay near you."

They were coming to the bend in the cave.

The four children were walking together.

Mrs. Tandy and Chief Hemster were walking behind.

The children turned the corner.

The cave floor went down on a deep slant.

Sammy held on tight to the wheel chair to keep it from rolling down.

"Boy," he whispered. "This would be great for a skate-board in here."

There was a faint gray light at the end of the cave.

They all shined their lights at that end.

"Holy Cow!"

"Holy Smoke!"

"Good Grief!"

"My Gosh!"

They forgot to whisper. They all shouted.

Mrs. Tandy and Chief Hemster ran around the bend in the cave.

Here's what they saw:

In front of them was an under-ground lake. Near the far wall was a high, flat rock as big as a room. On it sat a man, and a young woman holding a little child.

Next to them was a cat and four kittens. And the gang's corn pot. And a pile of note books and papers.

Slowly the man got up. He walked toward them, to the edge of the rock.

He was a little, thin, white-haired man. His skin was tan. His dark eyes looked sad.

He said, "I am Tran Lee. My daughter's child is sick. We have run out of food. I pray you will help us."

Then he fell in a faint.

The woman on the rock screamed.

Her father had fallen into the underground lake.

XI—The Rescue

BILL WAS PULLING off his shoes and pants.

"Come on, gang," he said. "Let's get him out!"

Sammy was down to his under pants by

the time the chief had his gun belt off.

Kathy was first to jump into the water. She shouted to the boys, "Don't dive. Come in feet first. You might hit your head on a rock."

The three of them swam across the water.

The man was moving around now. He was trying to keep his head above water.

His daughter was leaning over the rock. She was crying. But she could not help save him. She could not leave her child alone on the rock.

Her cries made an echo in the cave room.

Mrs. Tandy stayed with Dave. She helped him keep his chair from slipping down into the lake. He set his chair brakes.

Chief Hemster was in the water now, too. He was helping the children keep Mr. Lee's head up.

Dave was calling directions to them.

He shouted, "Swim to your right. There's a rock you can grab right near the edge of the water.

"There's a flat place right here next to it."

The shouting scared the little boy. He started crying.

Ghosty started to meow.

Her kittens got scared and they started in, too.

Echoes rang around the cave.

It sounded as if fifty people were talking at once.

At last they got Mr. Lee out of the water. He was all right.

But how would they get to his daughter on the rock? She was smiling now . . . she saw her father was safe.

Dave called to her, "Stay right there. We have a rubber raft in the car. We'll blow it up and . . . !"

Mr. Lee interrupted him. "No, no," he said. "There is another way out of this cave. There is a thin door-way behind that rock."

He pointed to the wall in back of his daughter. He said, "My daughter knows how to get out."

Dave said, "Wait a minute. I've been making a map of these caverns in my mind.

"I have a feeling that that's the same side of the hill our cave door is on."

Mr. Lee said, "Yes, it is. In fact our little door way is not twenty feet from your cave opening.

"We're just a little further up the road behind some bushes."

Sammy said, "So that's how you popped in and stole our corn."

Kathy and Bill both poked him to keep him quiet.

Sammy said, "Stop poking me, you two brats."

Mrs. Tandy said, "Look here, every body, we have things to do.

"First, every one had better stop running around in his under wear! You'll catch your death of cold! And throw on your coats, too."

The four of them, Chief Hemster, Kathy, Bill and Sammy, looked down at their legs.

Kathy turned bright red.

They all ran over and pulled on their jeans.

Sammy yelled, "Why didn't you say some thing sooner, Mrs. Tandy! I've been standing there in front of strangers with out my pants!"

Bill laughed.

Sammy yelled, "You should have reminded me, Bill. It's your fault."

Bill just laughed again.

Sammy grabbed Bill's shoe and pretended he was going to throw it into the water.

Dave called across to the young woman,

"Go to the door of your cave. We'll go back through the caves and meet you with an umbrella. We'll bring some thing warm to wrap the baby."

Kathy added, "And I'll bring a box for the kittens."

The woman didn't seem to understand them.

Then her father began to talk to her in a language that was not English.

She nodded and walked toward the back wall.

Sammy said, "Hey! What was that? Chinese? Hey! How many languages do you know?"

Bill said, "We'll find out about all that later. We'd better go get his daughter."

Sammy made an awful face at Bill. "OK, big bossy brat brother."

Then he said, "I'll walk with you Mr. Lee. You can just lean on me. I'm the strongest one in the gang. I'm MUCH stronger than Bill."

They got Mr. Lee back to their cave. They wanted him to lie down in a sleeping bag and wait for them.

Mr. Lee said, "Oh no, no. I must be sure all the papers are saved."

So they all put on their rain coats.

They gave Mr. Lee a warm coat.

They took a box and a blanket.

They ran out side to Mr. Lee's cave door.

In a few minutes they came back.

Mr. Lee had his arms full of note books and papers.

Mrs. Tandy was carrying the baby.

Kathy was carrying a box full of kittens.

The chief was helping Mr. Lee's daughter.

Bill carried Ghosty inside his coat.

And Sammy was carrying the pot of corn.

Dave had stayed behind. He had the camp stove going.

Then Sammy put the pot on it.

He said, "This is the biggest rescue we've ever made.

"We've got a man, a woman, a baby, a cat, four kittens, and twelve ears of corn."

Mr. Lee said, "My family were so cold and hungry, I stole your food. I am so sorry."

Mrs. Tandy said, "Don't think another thing about it.

"Here are some dry clothes of Dave's. Put them on. They'll be too long, but you can roll up the arms and legs.

"Then come over here and start in on this left-over chicken."

She handed some to his daughter.

She began to gulp it down like a hungry puppy.

Mrs. Tandy poured out a cup of milk and fed it to the little boy.

He loved it and the cookie she gave him.

Sammy leaned over to look at him closely.

The baby pushed his wet cookie right into Sammy's mouth.

Sammy cried, "Yuck!"

Every one laughed, even Mr. Lee.

Chief Hemster said, "Well, it looks like we are all feeling well enough to find out about each other. Mr. Lee, tell us how you ended up on a rock above a lake in a cave?"

XII—The Boat People

Mr. Lee said, "First let me thank you. I must find out who you are. Some day I hope my daughter Hong and I will be able to pay you back for your kindness."

Sammy said, "I'm Sammy Westburg.

These are my brother and sister, Bill and Kathy."

Bill said, "These are Dave Briggs and Becky Tandy, our best friends. We all live together. We five are the Woodland Gang. That's what we call our selves."

Mrs. Tandy said, "This is John Hemster. He's the chief of police from our town."

Sammy added, "He's a very good friend of ours. And he likes Mrs. Tandy a LOT!"

Chief Hemster said, "Now tell us how you got into the trouble we found you in."

They all sat on covers on the cave floor.

Mr. Lee said, "I am from Viet Nam.

"I was in charge of farming in all of South Viet Nam.

"We were at war with North Viet Nam.

They were communists. They wanted to rule us.

"Early in the war my wife and three children were staying with my mother. The North Viet Nam people over-ran the town. Then United States army men over-ran the town.

"I was told that all my family were killed."

Mrs. Tandy said, "Oh my. You poor man." She put her hand on his arm.

Sammy said, "That's terrible. I hate that!"

Dave said, "But you called Hong your daughter. Then she isn't your daughter?"

Mr. Lee said, "I'll answer that in a minute. But first let me tell you how I got here.

"I had lost my whole family. I felt I could not go on with my work.

"But others had lost their families too. And my country needed me.

"I kept on with planning the planting of crops. I arranged to buy the foods we needed from other countries. We had to feed our people.

"But we lost the war. The communists won. Then I had to leave my country. Some friends helped me escape. I would have been killed if I had stayed.

"After many years I got to the United States. That was six years ago."

Dave asked, "How did you learn to speak English so well?"

Mr. Lee said, "When I was a child we learned it in school. Then when I worked for my country I spoke it with people from the United States.

"Now I am a citizen of this great country. It has given me a new life."

Mrs. Tandy said, "Mr. Lee, how do you live here? How do you earn money?"

He answered, "As a lad I lived on a farm. Here I went to work for a flower

grower, in the fields.

"Then I worked in his green house.

"Now, I work here for the U. S. Park System. I'm in charge of re-planting meadow land."

Chief Hemster said, "Then what in the world are you doing living in a cave? You must earn enough money to rent an apartment!"

Mr. Lee said, "A year ago I heard from some one who used to live in my mother's town. Now he lives in the United States, too.

"He told me about a young woman in the boat he had escaped in two years ago.

"She had been from my mother's town too.

"She had been away playing in the fields when her family was killed. She was only four years old.

"She came back and found them dead. She ran away.

"She could no longer remember her name or the names of her family. The shock of finding them dead had been too much for her.

"All she could remember was the name of her town.

"For many years she begged for food from door to door.

"She grew older. She worked on a farm for her food.

"At last she met and married a young farmer.

"Soon they found a baby was on the way. They decided to run away from their country to a free land. They wanted their child to be born free.

"They made plans with twenty-two other people.

"Then in the dark of night, they all took a fishing boat. They put food and water into it.

"Quietly they pushed the boat off from the land.

"They used long poles to move it away from shore without noise. They held their breaths. They were afraid.

"They rowed their boat out into the

ocean. They knew they might die, but they wanted so much to be free, they took their chance.

"They were at sea for many days. Their food ran out. Some of them got sick and died.

"Hong's young husband was one of those."

Hong heard her father say her name. She smiled at her new friends. Kathy got up and went over to her.

She sat down next to her and put her arm around her.

Kathy was crying.

Mr. Lee said, "Hong and ten of the others were saved by a Swedish ship. When I heard about her, she was in Sweden. She had her baby. And she had named him Tran, the same name as mine."

Dave said, "Do you think she remem-

bered your name through all the years?"

Mr. Lee said, "I don't know. She may have used the name only by chance. I don't even know for sure if she is my daughter by birth. But she had lost her family. I had lost my family. All I had to love was my cat.

"I took all my savings out of the bank. My boss, the head ranger here, loaned me more money.

"The cave mapping crew needed some one to stay with their things at night. They were working in a lower cave room.

They gave the job to me. That way I wouldn't have to pay rent for my apartment. I could pay back my loan sooner."

Dave asked, "Why didn't they use the cavern we are in?"

Mr. Lee said, "The Devil's Deep Freeze Caves aren't open for use. But some times tough gangs have used this cavern, the one you are camped in.

"So the park crew decided not to use it. They were afraid their things might be hurt or stolen. In the day time they were further inside the cave, and I was not in it.

"The opening to the one we used is much harder to find. It was safer."

Dave said, "I bet that's why you didn't come to us for help right away. You thought we might be a bad gang hiding in here."

Mr. Lee said, "Yes, you're right."

Sammy asked, "What happened next?"

Mr. Lee said, "Then I hired a lawyer. He began to help me adopt Hong. At last he did it!

"Ten days ago Hong and the baby flew to the United States. I moved them into my cave home. The cat had her kittens. We made her a leafy nest. Now I had a daughter and grand son. We were a family at last."

Sammy said, "But where IS your cave home? Why were you on a rock above a lake?"

Mr. Lee answered, "My cave home is now under the lake!"

Bill said, "Holy Cow! You mean you were flooded out?"

Mr. Lee said, "This is the worst rain I've ever seen in this park. The water must have been too heavy on the stone floor above the cave.

"Some where it broke through. It poured into our room in the night. Every thing I owned is gone. All I saved were my family and cats, and the papers I was guarding for the park. I would have lost those, too. But my good cat went MEOW so loudly she woke me in time.

"It is lucky she had moved with her kittens back to our cave early last night. She must have been a little worried that you would take her babies.

"Our food is all gone, floating in the lake.

"My tent is gone. All the clothes I bought for Hong and little Tran are lost. All my clothing and books, every thing, gone.

"I've worked my hardest, but I have failed."

They were all quiet.

Then Sammy jumped up from where he sat.

He began waving his fists in the air. He said, "Darn this rain. Darn that war. You didn't fail at all. That's a bunch of hog wash, Mr. Lee. You're a hero! And so is Ghosty!"

Bill said, "Sammy's right. I hate to say it, but Sammy's perfectly right. You didn't fail at all. You won!"

Dave said, "Hey gang, come here for a minute."

They all gathered around him, like players in a foot ball huddle. So did the chief.

They listened to him for a minute. Then Dave wheeled over to Mr. Lee.

He said, "You've worked alone and bravely long enough, Mr. Lee. Now the Woodland Gang is stepping in to help."

XIII—A New Start

KATHY, SHY, QUIET Kathy, spoke up. "We have a lot of different things to do."

She took a pencil and paper out of her back pack.

"I'm going to write them down.

"First, we have to tell the park chief

about Mr. Lee saving the mapping papers. And how brave he was to do it in the dark flood.

"We have to see if they want him to set up camp in our cave now. Maybe they can put up a door for the time being."

Mr. Lee said, "How kind of you. But I have no things to camp here with now."

Sammy said, "Don't worry. I'll think of some thing."

Mrs. Tandy broke in. "I'm going to take charge of the clothes. First I will find a doctor to check baby Tran.

"Then I'm taking Hong and little Tran out on a shopping spree. What fun for me!"

Mr. Lee told Hong what Mrs. Tandy had said. She clapped her thin little hands in excitement.

Kathy added "Buy clothes" to the list.

Bill said, "Hey, this was the last camping trip we were planning for a couple of months. It's too wet out side to do much. Let's go home today.

"Then we can lend our tent and some other camping things to Mr. Lee until he moves back into an apartment."

Sammy said, "Why you little blabber mouth. That's just what I was going to think of."

Kathy wrote, "Divide our things, to leave camping things for Mr. Lee."

Mr. Lee said, "You are too kind. How can I take such help from strangers? I can do nothing to pay you back."

Mrs. Tandy said, "Why Mr. Lee, it's our good luck that we are able to help you.

"Some day when you are back on your feet, you'll help some one else. And you'll think of us. That will be pay enough."

Dave said, "I think the rain has let up,

Gang. Let's get going on this list."

Mrs. Tandy drove off out of the park with Hong and the baby, on the great clothes hunt.

Kathy and Dave stayed in the cave. They decided what to leave for Mr. Lee's family. They packed up the things they would take in the car.

Dave said, "Let's leave every bit of food. They can use it to start up again."

Kathy said, "That's a good idea. And let's leave three sleeping bags and three air mattresses. It will be getting cold soon, and they'll need them.

"And our camp stove for hot food."

Dave said, "We'd better leave a couple of pots and pans, too."

Bill, Sammy, Mr. Lee and Chief Hemster, went to the park's chief ranger.

Mr. Lee was carrying Bill's back pack.

Mr. Lee said sadly, "Mr. Wills, I have some thing terrible to report. All your tools for mapping are lost. I could not save them, no matter how hard I tried."

Mr. Wills said, "Good heavens, Tran! What happened to your park clothes? Why are you wearing some body's rolled up jeans?

"And who are these people?"

Sammy got mad. His wet hair stuck out all over his head like tooth picks. His eyes crossed.

He yelled, "Hey! You sound like you're mad at Mr. Lee. And you shouldn't be.

He's a hero! And we are too! And so is his cat!

"And this is Chief Hemster. He's a police man. And you'd better be careful or you're under arrest!"

At these last words, Mr. Wills and Chief Hemster and Bill all began to laugh.

Even Mr. Lee smiled through his sad look.

Mr. Wills said, "I'm not mad, son. I know how brave Mr. Lee is. I was just worried about him."

Then Mr. Lee told him about the flood and the under-ground lake.

When he was done, Mr. Lee said, "I hope I can still be your guard."

He told Mr. Wills about the idea of adding a door and moving into the other cave.

Mr. Wills said, "I'd love to say yes, Tran. But you see, we can't start the mapping all over again.

"I'm afraid we will have to shut down those caves until we can get more money."

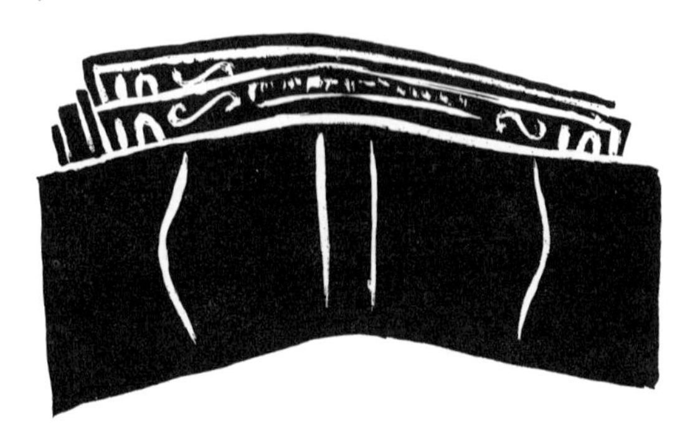

Bill said, "But don't you have insurance to pay for new tools?"

Mr. Wills said, "Oh yes. But with all our work papers lost, we would have to begin over. It would take too long. Our money would run out."

Bill said, "Wait a minute! Mr. Lee, open up that back pack. The papers aren't lost, Mr. Wills."

Sammy said, "Only the tools are gone. Look what Mr. Lee saved."

Mr. Wills took one long look at the papers inside.

Then he yelled, "Yippee! Tran, of course you can stay on with your family in the other cave! You've saved all our months of work. We can go right on with it." He grabbed Mr. Lee to hug him.

Then Mr. Lee hugged Sammy, and in a second every one was hugging and shaking hands.

Sammy got so excited, he even hugged Bill.

"Well," said Mr. Lee, "I want to go back and tell Hong the news. My family has a brand new start."

They drove back with Mr. Wills. Kathy and Dave were waiting.

They took lanterns and showed Mr. Wills the new under ground lake.

Then they heard the station wagon drive up. They went to meet Mrs. Tandy, Hong, and Little Tran. Mrs. Tandy had fourteen different bags and boxes for them to carry in.

Next the gang fixed up the cave for the Lees to live in.

Then Dave wheeled over to a card board box. He pulled out a big bag and a carton of milk.

He said, "Now here's a surprise Kathy and I have planned."

Kathy gave every one a napkin, and a paper cup full of milk.

Dave emptied the bag out onto a plate.

"Here they are," he said. "Our two day supply of oat meal cookies for a cave-warming party for the Lee's new home. We don't have to save any of them. We are going back home today."

They all sat down on the cave floor.

They ate those crunchy cookies and drank their cool milk.

And the biggest cookie of all, in a bowl of milk, went to Ghosty, the hero cat.